SPACE CASE

adapted by Kirsten Larsen
from the screenplay by Rob Hoegee
illustrated by Robert Roper

Ready-to-Read

Simon Spotlight
New York   London   Toronto   Sydney

Based on the TV series *Totally Spies!*™ created by
Marathon Animation as seen on Cartoon Network®.
Series created by Vincent Chalvon-Demersay, David Michel,
and Stéphane Berry

SIMON SPOTLIGHT
An imprint of Simon & Schuster Children's Publishing Division
1230 Avenue of the Americas, New York, New York 10020

Library of Congress Cataloging in Publication Data
Larsen, Kirsten.
Space case / adapted by Kirsten Larsen ; illustrated
by Robert Roper.
p. cm. – (Ready-to-read)
"Totally spies!"
"From the screenplay by Rob Hoegee."
"Based on the TV series Totally Spies! created by
Marathon Animation as seen on Cartoon Network."
ISBN-13: 978-1-4169-1571-3
ISBN-10: 1-4169-1571-0
I. Roper, Robert. II. Hoegee, Rob. III. Totally spies!
(Television program) IV. Title. V. Series.
PZ7.L323817Sqs 2006
2006007687

The spies were excited!

They had a new house

where they could live on their own.

"No parents! No rules!" said Sam.

"We can do whatever we want!"

added Clover.

"Ahem!" someone said.

The spies turned around and saw

a woman they did not know.

"Who are you?" asked Clover.

"I am Mrs. Beesbottom,

your nanny," the woman said.

The spies were angry.

"We do **not** need a nanny!"

they told Jerry.

"Do not worry about that now," said Jerry. "Meteors have been hitting Earth. You must find out why."

Jerry showed the spies
the gadgets for their mission.
"These magnetic boots will help
you walk on metal," he said.

"This perfume will freeze whatever you spray it on," Jerry told the spies. "And here is a remote beeper to call your nanny."

The spies took a rocket ship
to outer space.
They saw a burning meteor
headed for Earth.

Clover and Alex put on the
magnetic boots.
Standing on the rocket,
they threw the perfume
at the meteor.

The meteor froze just before
it crashed into Earth!
It barely missed hitting
some astronauts at a training school.

"Hmm . . . the meteor seemed to be targeting astronauts," Sam said.

The spies traced the meteor

to an old space station.

No one lived there anymore.

"This space station is not safe,"

said Sam.

"It could burn up any minute."

Inside the space station

the spies met a strange woman.

Alex recognized her.

"Miss Lady Luna!" said Alex.

"You tell fortunes on TV!"

The spies found out that
Miss Lady Luna was sending
meteors to hit astronauts.
She was angry.
"I wanted to be part of the
space station crew," she said,
"but I did not get picked."

Her next target was Ricky Rickerson, a pop singer and an astronaut. Miss Lady Luna was going to send a meteor to destroy him!

Miss Lady Luna blew stardust
at the spies.

"I can't see!" cried Alex.

Then Miss Lady Luna stole
their rocket ship.

Now the spies were trapped
aboard the space station!

Sam punched a hole in the wall of the space station. All of the dust gushed out into space.

But the spies still had a problem.
They did not have a way to get
back to Earth!

The spies had to call their nanny,

who came to rescue them in a jet.

"I am very disappointed,"

said Mrs. Beesbottom.

Mrs. Beesbottom dropped the spies off
over Los Angeles.

Now it was time
to rescue Ricky Rickerson!

They got there just in time!
The spies swooped in
and grabbed Ricky.
A second later the meteor
crashed into Earth!

Miss Lady Luna was watching.

"You have ruined everything!"

she cried.

"It looks like you are going
to jail," said Clover.
But Miss Lady Luna escaped.
"Let's go get her!" said Sam.

The spies chased after
Miss Lady Luna.
They had almost caught her
when she blasted them with
a beam of sunlight.

"I have star power!"

said Miss Lady Luna.

"And the sun is the most

powerful star!"

Just then the sun set,

and Miss Lady Luna lost her power.

"It looks like someone pulled

the plug on you," Sam said.

When the spies got home that night,
their house was empty.

"Where is the nanny?" asked Alex.

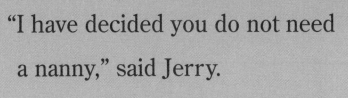

"I have decided you do not need
a nanny," said Jerry.
"You'll do fine on your own."
"Hooray!" the spies cheered.